My friend Percy and the Sheik

My friend Percy and the Sheik

Ulf Stark

 GECKO PRESS

Also by Ulf Stark
Can you whistle, Johanna?
(GECKO PRESS, 2005)
My friend Percy's magical gym shoes
(GECKO PRESS, 2005)

This translation published with the assistance of Svenska Institutet (SI)

©Ulf Stark 1995
First published in Sweden by Bonnier Carlsen Bokförlaget, Stockholm, Sweden
Published in the English language by arrangement with
Bonnier Carlsen Bokförlaget
Original title: *Min vän shejken i Stureby*

This edition first published in 2006 by
Gecko Press, PO Box 9335, Marion Square, Wellington 6141, New Zealand
English translation © Gecko Press 2006

Cataloguing-in-Publication Data for this title is available
from the National Library of New Zealand

ISBN: 0-9582720-1-8

Cover design: Sarah Maxey
Typesetting: Archetype
Printed by Everbest

For more curiously good books, visit www.geckopress.com
or email gecko@geckopress.com

Contents

CHAPTER ONE

A boxing glove in your face

"A good book grabs you right from the first page. It can make you laugh and cry. And nothing in the world will make you stop reading it," Dad said one afternoon, just when Ulf was getting ready to go out.

He was standing in the hall in his white dentist coat, holding a thick book he had taken from the shelf called *The Count of Monte Christo*. You could smell the dust and complicated words a mile off.

"This is a French book," he said. "You should read it."

"No," said Ulf.

"If you don't read anything, you'll never learn anything," said Dad.

"No," said Ulf.

And he shot out the door.

He was off to meet his friends Percy, Olle Rickberg and Charlie. That's what he did every day. No book in the world was going to make him stay at home on a day like this, with the sun shining and the chance to do target practice with an air gun at Bjorn's place.

Ulf sniffed the newly-baked bread as he ran past the bakery. At the corner he threw a sugar cube from his pocket at the snappy fox terrier, like he always did.

Down the street he went, arms out. He was a Flying Barrel, which is the name of a short and chubby aeroplane. The name suited Ulf because he was chubby himself.

When he saw the others waiting at the end of the street he put his wings down.

Percy was eating a green apple, Charlie was tugging at his ear and Olle Rickberg was looking at his new Certina watch.

"You're late," he said.

"Yeah, I was talking to Dad," said Ulf. "Let's go!"

The air gun was at Bjorn's. It was a Diana. Usually they shot coloured arrows at pictures they cut out from magazines.

But today they didn't even get to the gate.

Lasse Agren was standing outside Doctor Andrén's with a nasty grin on his round face.

"Hello ya little snot faces," he said.

Lasse was a couple of years older than Ulf and his friends, and he weighed at least 20 kilos more. He and his brother Hadar owned a pair of boxing gloves made from real pigskin. They took turns with them. One week Hadar would have the right-hand glove and Lasse would have the left. The next week they'd swap.

You had to watch out on the weeks when it was Lasse's turn with the right-hand glove. Lasse was strong, and he had a good eye.

He grabbed hold of Ulf and pushed the glove up under his nose till he could smell pig.

"Have you seen this?" he said.

"Ye-es," said Ulf. "Nice glove."

"And hard," Lasse sniggered. "D'ya want to taste it?"

"No, thank you," said Ulf. "I already have."

The year before, Ulf would have hit him straight off, because then he had a pair of magical gym shoes. But he'd burned them. So now he took a step back towards Doctor Andrén's rooms.

"Lay off!" shouted Percy. "Leave Ulf alone! He's practically my brother. You'll be sorry if you touch him!"

"Whaddid he say?" Lasse grunted.

"Nothing," said Ulf. "What would you like today?"

"Buns," said Lasse.

So they all went to the bakery opposite Ulf's house.

Every morning Ulf sniffed the euphoric smells of dough, cardamom and cinnamon as he set off for school.

"Come on, let's go in," said Lasse. "You can put it on your mother's account."

He went round the little shop with his nostrils flaring. He looked at the shelves, loaded with Danish pastries. There were cardamom rings, biscuits and tiger cookies. When he had finished looking, he punched Ulf in the side.

"This one!" he hissed. "And these ones. And these!"

He nodded at a fresh loaf, some small cookies and three wonderful Dresden waffles. And Ulf said in a squeaky voice that he would like them all and that they should go on his mother's account.

"Ah ha, so Mrs Stark is having visitors?" Miss Larsson asked as she took the waffles down from the shelf.

"Yes," said Lasse. "Except today she has a migraine."

With the bread and cakes in a brown paper bag, Lasse went across the street. He sat down behind the big stone in the clearing where you couldn't be seen. Sometimes the men from the old people's home sat there drinking beer. But now Lasse leaned on the stone, and had his own party with the small cakes, the Dresden waffles and the very long loaf.

"Mmm, yum. Fantastic," he said.

Ulf and the others were silent. They watched the bread disappear into Lasse's mouth. They didn't get to taste even a little bit, because when Lasse couldn't fit any more in, he threw the rest to the birds.

"Sheez, I'm full," he said. "But I'll soon be hungry again."

He crunched up the paper bag, waved, and went away.

"Woah, he's got a big stomach," said Charlie. "I wonder how come he doesn't pop."

"I wonder what my mother will say," said Ulf.

They went back to Bjorn's place to shoot with the air gun. But it wasn't much fun. Ulf missed almost every shot.

"You never shoot this badly," said Percy. "What's the matter?"

"I wonder what Lasse will want next time," said Ulf.

Every time Lasse was wearing the right-hand glove he wanted something. Once it was Ulf's best yo-yo. Another time he took the false teeth Ulf's father gave him which made a terrible smile when you put them in your mouth.

"This can't go on," said Percy. "We'll have to think of something."

"Yeah, something clever," said Olle Rickberg.

"I was going to say that," said Charlie.

So they each went home to think of something clever.

CHAPTER TWO

Ulf reads a good book

It wasn't too long before Ulf's mother discovered he had put the buns and cakes on her account at the bakery.

"But darling," she said, the next evening as they drank hot chocolate and ate sandwiches. "How could you do something so incredibly stupid?"

"I don't know," said Ulf. "I was just hungry. I didn't think about it."

"He doesn't think," said Jan.

Jan was Ulf's brother. He was older and thinner than Ulf.

"But we have thousands of buns at home," said his mother. "I felt like an idiot when Miss Larsson asked me if my coffee morning had gone well."

"He eats too much," said Jan. "That's his problem. And he makes smacking noises when he eats."

Dad said something in French. And he said that the

cost of the buns would be deducted from Ulf's pocket money.

Then he went downstairs to his radio equipment.

Ulf's father was a radio amateur. He spent the weekends and evenings talking to other amateurs around the world. He talked into his microphone in Stureby and they could hear his voice from their loudspeakers in New Guinea or Australia. Then they sent each other cards called QSL cards. Around the world radio people were friends and called each other strange names, like DL 1 KW or ZC 12 AA.

Ulf's father was called SM 5 FL.

After a while Ulf went downstairs too.

He sat quietly on the sofa. When his father was talking on his radio, he and Jan had to be quiet.

Ulf thought about life and about Lasse. He listened to his father talking into the microphone, and to the squeaks and rasps coming from the radio receiver.

"Hallo! Hallo! This is SM 5 FL," said Dad.

"Are you talking to Greenland?" Ulf asked.

"No, I am trying to make contact with Saudi Arabia," said Dad, turning the dials feverishly.

"You know, Dad," said Ulf. "There's something I'm thinking about."

He looked at his father in his grey cardigan sitting at the desk with the world globe lamp shining on it. Ulf was thinking that he should tell him what had really happened with the buns. And then his father would come and sit down beside him on the sofa, with his dentist smell, and tell him exactly what he should do.

"What's that?" muttered his father. "What are you thinking about?"

"About life," said Ulf.

"Yeah, yeah," said Dad. "But right now you have to be quiet. I am sending, as you can see. Get yourself a book to look at for a moment."

So Ulf did.

There were lots of books in his father's bookshelf. There was *The Count of Monte Christo*. There was *Mutiny on the Bounty*, another of his father's favourites. And there was the one about how to bring up your children. But the one Ulf picked up and leafed through was called *My Father is a Cannibal*. In it there were photographs of naked pygmy-women covered in pig fat with bones in their hands.

He had looked at it a thousand times, so after a while he got tired of it. He picked up a book he hadn't seen before. It had a green spine and was called *The Basics of Hypnosis*.

It was a thick book, full of very small words.

When he started to read it, he realised it was a good book. It grabbed him right from the start. Then he couldn't stop reading it.

He forgot about the women covered in pig fat. He forgot about his father and the voices coming from his apparatus. He had the feeling that this book could be really useful.

So as it got darker and darker he sat on the sofa, reading. He looked at the pictures of people lying on their beds, while the person hypnotising them swung something that looked like Dad's gold watch, in front of their swimmy eyes.

"But dear boy," said his father, about to turn off the downstairs lights. "Are you still here? Aren't you going up to bed?"

"Soon," mumbled Ulf. "I'm just going to finish this book. I've only got eighty-nine pages left to go."

His father gave him a hug.

"Don't stay up too long," he said.

"I won't," said Ulf.

But he did.

He stayed there till he fell asleep on the sofa with his head on his father's black cushion and *The Basics of Hypnosis* on his chest.

CHAPTER THREE

Lasse gets a cracker on his loaf

One afternoon two weeks later Ulf said to Percy, Charlie and Olle Rickberg that he wanted to go to Bjorn's house to shoot targets with his air gun.

"Are you crazy?" said Olle Rickberg. "Lasse will get us for sure."

"Yeah, and this week he has the right-hand glove again," Charlie pointed out, tugging anxiously at his ear.

"What's it matter?" said Ulf. "He might not be there. And we're not scared of him, are we?"

"Nah, Ulf's right," said Percy. "We shouldn't let that knucklehead decide what we do."

So off they went to Bjorn's house.

Ulf put his hand in his pocket to make sure. There it was, his father's gold watch. While he fingered the cold metal he repeated to himself the words he'd been reading in the book with the green spine.

Last night he had tried it out on Olle Rickberg's boxer, when he took him out for a pee. It went well. The dog yawned and lay on his back straight away. Except that he was an expert at sleeping, and Lasse wasn't.

"What are you muttering about?" Charlie asked.

"Nothing," said Ulf.

And they carried on towards Bjorn's. Sure enough, Lasse was waiting for them behind a power pole, with his brown boxing glove with the word FIGHTER on it.

"Hello ya little snotfaces," he said stepping forward. "I knew you'd all come along sooner or later."

"Yes, we wanted so much to see you again," said Ulf.

Lasse looked around in case they'd brought a grown-up with them. He thought they were trying to trick him, and he hated being tricked.

"Why's that?" he said, screwing up his eyes.

"Because now I'm going to hypnotise you," said Ulf.

"No, you're not," said Lasse. "It's time for my buns. Come on; we're going to the bakery."

He slapped his boxing glove against his stomach to show how hungry he was. Boof-boof, it went. It made the same sound as when he trampled caps in the mud.

"He's chicken," said Percy.

"That's what I was going to say," said Charlie.

Lasse's cheeks went red. If there was anything he didn't like it was being called chicken. Then he would do anything. Once he ate up two stinkflies. Another time he sat for half an hour in an anthill with no trousers on.

"I'm not chicken," he said. "But Ulf's lying. He can't trick me. He can't do it. And if he can't do it then he'll get a cracker on his loaf!"

Lasse followed them round to the back of Bjorn's house because Ulf said that was the best place to be hypnotised. There was an empty rabbit hutch left over from the war, a swing, and a pine tree. There was a compost heap under the pine tree for leaves and grass and kitchen scraps.

Ulf pointed at the tree, to a branch quite high up.

"You have to climb up there," he said. "And hang from your knees."

"What for?" said Lasse.

"Because a person being hypnotised has to have their head low," said Ulf. "Everybody knows that."

So Lasse climbed onto the compost heap and up the tree.

"Are you ready?" Ulf shouted, after a bit.

"Yes!" Lasse shouted back. "Now get on with it!"

Ulf pulled the gold watch out of his pocket. It had a gold chain too. His father usually put it on his waistcoat when he went with Grandpa to Odd Fellows. But now Ulf let it swing backwards and forwards on its chain.

"Can you see the watch?" shouted Ulf. "You have to watch it the whole time and not let it out of your sight for a single second."

The gold watch caught the afternoon sun. It cast glittery reflections everywhere. Lasse couldn't take his eyes off it.

"You're feeling more and more tired," Ulf droned in the sleepy monotone he had been practising in the toilet. "Your body is getting heavier and heavier. Your head is heavy. Your legs are heavy. Your stomach is very heavy. All of you is getting more and more relaxed. And you are breathing all the time with big, deep breaths."

They could hear him puffing up in the tree.

"I'm going to count to twenty," Ulf droned. "When I get to twenty you'll fall into a deep and comfortable sleep."

Lasse fell asleep at eighteen.

He fell right into the compost. He lay there quite still, buried in coffee grounds and old potato peelings. Percy, Charlie and Olle Rickberg walked cautiously over and looked at him. Ulf put his father's gold watch back into his pocket.

"Wow, that was beautiful," said Charlie. "You're as good as Mandrake, you are."

"All I did was read a book," said Ulf.

He leaned over Lasse. He could hear him breathing. After a while he saw one of Lasse's eyelids twitch.

"Can you wake him?" asked Olle Rickberg.

"I think so," said Ulf.

He put his mouth to Lasse's ear.

"YOU CAN WAKE UP NOW!" he shouted.

Lasse sat bolt upright. He put his hands on his head and looked at the swing swaying in the wind.

"How did I get here?" he asked. "What's happening?"

"You just had a little sleep," said Ulf. "You fell into a deep sleep, just like I said you would. Are you feeling a bit dizzy?"

"Yeah, my head's spinning," said Lasse.

"I know," said Ulf. "That often happens when you've been hypnotised. But now you know I wasn't tricking. And you know what will happen if you try to fight us again."

"Yes," said Lasse.

"You can go now," said Ulf.

"Yeah," said Percy. "But first you can buy us all a Snickers each."

They were about to go when Bjorn came out with the air gun and a pile of old magazines.

"Where are you going?" he asked. "I thought we were going to do shooting."

"Nah, we have to go to the sweet shop," said Percy. "Ulf has hypnotised Lasse, so now he's going to buy us Snickers."

CHAPTER FOUR

Ulf gets a kiss

The next day Lasse had a splendid egg on his head. All the kids clustered around Ulf when he got to school, looking at him with new eyes, while Percy and Charlie explained over and over what he had done to Lasse.

"He just lay there," said Percy. "You should have seen him. Like a dead whale. That's what Ulf can do with anyone if he wants!"

"With the headmaster as well?" Bengt's mouth was open.

"Easy peasy," said Charlie.

"And the school doctor when he squeezes you in the balls?"

"Sure," said Percy. "Anyone."

Then Ulf got two film star cards from Bengt: one with Roy Rogers in a brown cowboy hat and one with

Gina Lollobrigida in a low-cut dress. Percy took the one with the low-cut dress.

"As commission," he said. "I *am* going to be a businessman, you know."

"Yes, I know," said Ulf.

The school bell rang. Ulf was just about to go in when someone took his arm.

It was Marianne. He hadn't seen so much of her lately, because this year there was no foot phys ed. Their feet had graduated from foot phys ed now.

"Hi," she said. "Is it really true that you can hypnotise anybody you want to?"

"I think so," said Ulf.

"Can you do it to me?" she asked.

"Probably," said Ulf. "But you would have to look me in the eyes all the time."

"I could do that," she said. "Is this afternoon a good time?"

"Yes, it is," said Ulf. "We could meet over by the paddock, because I need to take Olle Rickberg's dog out for a walk anyway."

Then he ran off to the classroom with a spring in his step. When he arrived, the teacher was already handing out the maths tests she had corrected. Bengt was shining like a neon sign when he got his test back. But not Percy.

When the teacher said they had to take their tests home and that their parents had to sign them, Percy put up his hand.

"Dad is too tired to sign anything," he said. "He's very tired at the moment."

"Don't worry," said the teacher. "Soon we'll have another test and that one'll go better for you. You just have to try a bit harder. That makes all the difference."

"It won't help," said Percy. "I've already tried that."

"But maybe your father can help you?" said the teacher.

"Do you think so?" asked Percy.

"Of course," said the teacher. "If you ask him nicely."

"I'll ask him after dinner. He's usually in a better mood then," said Percy, smiling at all those squares and red pen marks.

After dinner Ulf ran off to collect Olle Rickberg's dog. It was a boxer called Peck with a wrinkled forehead and a tiny stump of a tail.

"If you wait a minute I can come with you," said Olle Rickberg.

"It's all right," said Ulf.

Then he ran as fast as he could down the street. Peck leapt around in front of him, waving his cut-off tail.

Marianne was already there when he got to the paddock. She was next to a rowanberry bush, in a dress with red spots. She had put her yellow hair into a ponytail with a rubber band. She smiled at him with her lovely, big front teeth.

"Hi," she said. "What do people do when they're going to be hypnotised?"

"They lie down," said Ulf and he tied Peck up to the rowanberry bush. "You can lie on the hill!"

He nodded towards a slope covered in buttercups, clover and daisies. Marianne lay down and looked up at the clouds.

"This is very comfortable," she said.

"Look me in the eyes the whole time," said Ulf.

"Like this?" she said, staring straight into his eyes with her grey-blue ones as he leaned over her.

"Ye-es," he said. "Just like that."

Then he had to blink, because it felt like he was looking straight at the sun.

"What will you make me do?" she asked.

"We'll see," said Ulf, because he hadn't thought about that. "Now you have to be quiet, because I'm going to start."

He told her to relax her whole body. And when she looked relaxed enough, he counted to twenty in his slow and sleepy hypnotising voice.

"Now it's almost done," he said. "Your eyelids will close now. You can't keep them open any longer. You're feeling comfortable and warm in your whole body. You are sort of floating away."

Ulf saw Marianne's eyes close.

"That's right," he said. "When I count backwards from ten to zero you'll wake up again. And when you wake up you will feel an irresistible need to press your lips against mine. Then you'll kiss me like you've never kissed before."

When Ulf got to zero, Marianne opened her eyes.

"Do you feel dizzy?" Ulf asked.

"Yes, I do. And a bit strange."

She stood up. They stood facing each other for a moment.

"Is there anything you feel like you need to do?" Ulf asked.

"I'm not sure," she said. "I don't really know what I'm doing."

Then she put her arms around his neck and pressed her soft lips against his. Ulf's crooked front tooth ground against her smooth teeth. It felt funny.

They stood there for a long time, holding each other. Then Peck started to bark because no one was throwing sticks for him.

Marianne woke up properly.

"Wow," she said.

"That's what I hypnotised you to do," said Ulf.

"I realise that," she said, "because I would never have done it otherwise. When will you hypnotise me again?"

"Soon," gasped Ulf. "But now I have to take Peck home to Olle Rickberg."

He licked his lips the whole way home.

Marianne walked beside him. She took him by the arm.

"What do you wish for most of all in the whole world?" she asked. She was licking her lips too.

"A dog," said Ulf.

Marianne let go of his arm.

CHAPTER FIVE

Percy becomes a genius

The next day they had to have X-rays taken. They had to take off their shirts and go into a white bus in the schoolyard to have their lungs photographed. The girls went in first and then the boys. They had to stand with their chests pressed against a cold metal plate and they couldn't move until the camera machine had stopped humming.

It didn't hurt a bit.

When they came out they ran to the person next in line and said it was the most horrible thing they'd ever done and that it felt as if their lungs would explode.

Ulf was smiling the whole time. He smiled even when the woman who took them into the bus told him to stop.

"It won't show up on the picture if that's what you're thinking," she said.

He pressed his chest hard against the plate and thought about how Marianne had pressed her chest against it before him.

After school they went off to climb some scaffolding. Ulf told Percy how well he'd done hypnotising Marianne.

"She did exactly as I told her," he said. "I am going to be a hypnotist when I grow up. Then I'll get to do a lot of really fun things like get people to crawl around on the floor and grunt because they think they're pigs."

"Yeah," sighed Percy. "I don't know what I want to be."

"Yes, you do," said Ulf. "You want to be a businessman. Have you forgotten?"

"Nah," said Percy. "It won't work."

"Why won't it work?"

"Because I can't do adding. That's what Dad said when I showed him my maths test. He said if I'm that bad at adding I'll never be a businessman."

"Didn't your Dad show you how then?" Ulf asked.

Percy didn't answer. He just kicked some stones along the road, and then Ulf didn't know what to say. So he kicked stones as well.

When they got to the bridge Ulf once walked over as if he was walking a tightrope, Percy suddenly perked up.

"That's a hell of a good idea!" he yelled. "I just thought of something."

"What?" asked Ulf.

"You can hypnotise me. Why didn't I think of it before? You can hypnotise anyone to do anything. So you can make me a mathematical genius."

"I'm not sure it will work," said Ulf.

"Of course it'll work," Percy grinned. "It worked on Lasse. It worked on Marianne. Why wouldn't it work on me? We might as well go home to my place right now."

So he took Ulf home to the yellow-grey apartment building on Bjule Street.

Inside, Percy's father was sitting in a nylon shirt and garters, smoking cigarettes from a packet which had Chesterfield on it.

He was tugging at his ear while he looked at a thick pile of papers on the kitchen table.

"Shh!" whispered Percy. "He mustn't be disturbed. Come on, let's go to my room."

So off they went. Percy closed the door carefully.

"Isn't your father out selling Venetian blinds?" Ulf asked.

"No, not today. He has so many things he has to add up. He's got some big business on the go at the moment."

"Will you be rich, then?"

"Yes," said Percy. "Then we'll buy a Saab, because Mum loves driving cars. And then she'll get a fur coat made from real Persian lambskin. Come on, let's get started!"

He lay down on the bed and looked Ulf in the eyes.

Ulf sat on a stool beside the bed and did what he usually did. He told Percy to relax in his whole body. And then he counted to twenty.

"Okay," mumbled Percy. "Now say that I'll be a mathematical genius!"

"When you wake up you'll be a mathematical genius," said Ulf.

Percy got up straight away and looked for his maths book, a pen and the sky-blue writing block in his school bag. He didn't think he'd need a rubber.

"Let's do it!" he said. "Let's do this one. It looks hard!"

He pointed to a sum in the book.

He wrinkled his forehead. He tugged his ear. Then he quickly wrote down some numbers. Then he came to a dead stop.

"What now?" he said. "What's this then? I still don't get it! You haven't tricked me, have you?"

He threw the pen against the wall.

"Nyah," said Ulf, picking up the pen. "But you have to practice before you can become a genius. I can sit here while you do it."

So they sat down together at Percy's desk and they looked at the sums in the book.

"You have to do division," said Ulf. "It's about the hardest thing there is. It's like you were going to give eighteen buns to six small kids. They all have to have the same number of buns. How many will each one get?"

"They won't be given any stupid buns," said Percy. "They'll have to buy them, three each, for cash. And if I get five cents for each bun that's ninety cents."

Ulf wrinkled his forehead. He had to do the sum on a piece of paper.

"You're right!" he said. "That's multiplication. You are becoming a mathematical genius, anyhow!"

They sat there for a while longer. Percy did sums till his head started to hurt.

"It's just sore from all the training," Ulf said. "That's enough for today. I have to go home for dinner."

Percy went with him almost the whole way home, because he needed some fresh air. He talked the whole way about his father's business, and how great it would be now he could help his father do his sums.

"See who's standing over there?" he whispered when they got to the big poplar trees on the corner.

Ulf saw.

Lasse was there, slapping his right-hand glove against a street light. Clonk-clonk, it went.

"Hey Lasse," Ulf called. "How're things?"

Lasse turned around and looked at them with tired eyes and his hands by his side.

"Not good actually," he muttered. "I don't know what to do anymore. It's boring. But jeez what a hiding you would have got if Ulf didn't know how to do hypnotising! I would have made him give me that gold watch. That would've been fun. I'd have turned both of you into jam."

"How?" asked Percy.

Then Lasse lifted up his boxing glove. He spun his arm round and round.

"Show us what you can do!" Percy called.

So Lasse did. He drove his hand into the street light as hard as he could. Then he hopped up and down and waved his hand around.

"Ouch!" he yelled. "Ouch, my wrist!"

"Unfortunately we need to get going now," said Ulf. "Bye Lasse."

They left quickly. Percy went with Ulf till they could see the house with the gigantic antennae on its roof. Then he stopped and said it would probably be best if he went home a different way.

"Thanks for today," he said, and patted Ulf on the back. "Today has been a good day."

"Tomorrow will be a good day too," said Ulf.

CHAPTER SIX

The power of hypnosis comes to an end

The next time they were waiting to get their maths tests back, Percy had been to the toilets and combed his hair with water. He didn't say a word about how he thought he'd done, even though Ulf had asked him a thousand times at least.

"I don't know," he said. "I just wrote and wrote like I was in a dream."

Now he was drumming his fingers on the desk top while the teacher handed out one test after another. At last she got to Percy.

"So it's just you left," she said.

"Ye-es," he said. "It didn't go very well, did it?"

"I don't know what to say," said the teacher.

Percy picked his nose.

"You don't have to say anything," he said. "I know it all went to hell. Just give it to me."

So the teacher gave him the test.

"I just want to say how pleased I am," she said. "Because this time you got them all right!"

Percy squirmed and turned the maths paper over to where there was a gold star and CONGRATULATIONS written in big red letters.

"Thanks," he said. "Thank you, miss!"

"Don't thank me," she smiled. "Thank yourself. But there's just one thing I don't understand."

"What's that?" Percy asked.

"The sums are all exactly right," said the teacher. "And the answers are all right too. But why in the world have you written DOLLARS and CENTS on every sum? Even when it's supposed to be LITRES and METRES?"

"Oh that," said Percy. "It's just a little trick Ulf showed me."

That afternoon Percy wanted to run home straight away to show the test to his father. But he was still waiting when Ulf came out into the yard.

He took Ulf's hand and shook it.

"Thanks," he said. "Without you I would never have become a genius."

"Aw, it was nothing," said Ulf.

"Course it was something," said Percy, "because now I can be a real businessman. And now I can help Dad with his sums. He'll be blown away!"

"Sure," said Ulf. "And pleased."

"Yeah," said Percy. "Do you want me to come home with you?"

"No, off you go," said Ulf.

He understood that Percy was in a hurry. And he had also seen Marianne coming with her school bag slung over one shoulder.

"See you tomorrow!" called Percy.

Then he was gone.

"Hi Ulf," Marianne said. "Shall we walk together a bit?"

"Yeah, why not," said Ulf.

So off they went under the blue summer sky and Ulf felt happy with Marianne walking beside him, because he had helped his best friend and because he was sure that now he could hypnotise anybody he wanted to.

At the end of the street Marianne put her arm in his. It felt fantastic. But it felt dangerous too, because he didn't want anyone to see and yell out 'girl-lover'.

"That was fun last time," said Marianne.

"Yeah," said Ulf.

"You promised you would hypnotise me again," she said. "Can you do it now?"

"It'll have to be quick," said Ulf, "because I have to get home in time for dinner."

They walked together to the park. They went past

the pond where toddlers were yelling and playing with their boats and splashing each other. Then they stopped behind a big maple tree with rustling leaves where no one could hear them.

"Shall I lie down?" asked Marianne.

"No, I haven't got time today," said Ulf. "This time you can stay standing up."

She stood with her back against the thick trunk. When he had counted to twenty her eyes shut by themselves.

"We might as well say the same thing as last time," he said.

"Nothing else?" she whispered in a quiet, dreamy voice.

He looked at her beautiful face, at the little frown between her eyes and at the lips he had already kissed. And he was thinking that she was just about as cute as a dog.

"Yeah," he whispered. "Soon you'll fall in love with a boy with blond hair, round cheeks and quite chubby thighs."

Later that evening Ulf was lying on the sofa downstairs, looking past the shiny mahogany door of his father's desk. He could see himself in it. What he saw was a guy with blond hair, round cheeks and quite chubby thighs.

He was as happy as anyone is who is thinking about kisses.

"Now I can do anything," he thought, licking his lips. "I can hypnotise anybody to do exactly what I want."

He got up.

He went to the desk where his father was sitting in his grey radio jersey with a pair of black earphones over his ears.

He leant forward and looked his father straight in the eyes. He had never looked this closely at his father before. His father's eyes were all sorts of colours: yellow and brown and green. And in the black pupils in the middle he could see himself upside down. Staring into his father's eyes felt uncomfortable.

"What is it?" his father said after a while, giggling. "Why are you staring at me like that? Are you not feeling well?"

"Yes," said Ulf. "But you are feeling more and more tired."

"What's that?" said his father, taking off his earphones.

"Soon you won't be able to keep your eyes open," continued Ulf. "When I've counted to twenty you will immediately fall asleep."

He counted to twenty while his father looked at him as if he thought Ulf was going crazy.

"There," said Ulf. "When you wake up again you'll feel an irresistible desire to get me my very own dog."

"Shhh!" hissed his father and started turning his dials.

"A collie would be best," said Ulf. "But a Newfoundland would also be good. Or a Gordon setter."

His father sighed. He turned off his radio apparatus. He wrinkled his forehead and didn't look the slightest bit hypnotised.

"Stop that Ulf," he muttered. "Because of your idiotics I've missed the man I've been waiting all night to talk to."

"Who's that?" asked Ulf.

"The sheik," said his father crossly. "Prince Talal Al Saud from Saudi Arabia."

Ulf was lying down and staring at the pictures from *Dog Sport* magazine he had stuck up on the wall with a stapler, when his father came in to say goodnight.

"You know, Dad," said Ulf. "Did you feel the slightest bit tired when I counted to twenty?"

"No, I didn't," said his father, and he still sounded cross.

"And you don't feel any desire to buy me a dog?"

"Not in the slightest."

"That's strange," said Ulf. "You can go now."

His father gave him a quick kiss on the cheek and went off to say goodnight to his brother.

Ulf lay there, listening to the wind in the trees. He thought about how he had lost his hypnotic power. Maybe he'd been using it too much.

He'd never get a dog now, he thought. But it was lucky that he had managed to hypnotise Marianne before it ran out. And it was lucky that he had hypnotised his best friend in time!

CHAPTER SEVEN

I'll have to start not liking it here now, says Percy

The next day Percy came late to school. He looked so tired that Ulf thought he must have sat up all night helping his father do his sums.

At morning break Percy didn't even want to go out. He was still sitting at his desk when Ulf came up to him.

"You seem a bit tired today," said Ulf.

"Maybe," said Percy. "Do I look tired?"

"You have black rings under your eyes," said Ulf. "You've been sitting up all night helping your father do his big business deal, haven't you?"

"Nah," he said. "I just couldn't sleep."

"Yeah, it can be like that when you're really happy," said Ulf. "But what did he say? He must've been blown away when you showed him your maths test, was he?"

"I don't want to talk about it now," said Percy.

"Then we'll wait till lunchtime," said Ulf.

At lunchtime, everyone rushed out as fast as they could to get to the shop and buy sweets and play football or knights.

For knights, one boy is a horse and piggybacks the other one who is the knight. Then you try to shove the other knights off till only one pair is left. Usually Ulf was the horse and Percy was the knight. It was a game they liked, because Percy was good at dragging the others off their horses.

But today they weren't in a hurry. They walked as slowly as they could to the dining room.

"So what's the story?" said Ulf. "Does your father think you can be a businessman now? What did he say?"

"He said I should never be a businessman," said Percy.

"WHAT?" said Ulf. "But you got the whole test right!"

"I know," said Percy. "He looked at it. And then he said I should never be a businessman. It's the worst job you can have, he said."

"How can he say that?" Ulf asked. "Right now when he's doing the business deal of his life and everything."

"It didn't come to anything," mumbled Percy looking down at the asphalt in the yard.

"Ach, it'll come right," said Ulf.

"No," said Percy. "It won't. Because no one wants to buy Dad's Venetian blinds in Stureby. Everybody has Venetian blinds here already. So now we have to move to Munkfors."

"He might change his mind," said Ulf.

Percy didn't think so. He had moved enough times to know when it was time. And in his father's sums there were only minuses, and his mother had already bought the Persian lambskin coat she had been dreaming about, because she believed so much in the big business deal. And now his father was sitting quietly with the atlas in front of him, thinking about where they should move to.

"The only thing would be if you could hypnotise him," said Percy when they went in to lunch. "Then maybe we could stay."

Ulf looked unhappily at Percy.

"I'm sorry Percy," he said. "I can't do hypnotism any more. My hypnotic powers have run out."

"Are you sure?" asked Percy.

"Afraid so," Ulf said.

Percy said nothing. They walked silently in. They stood in the queue for food. They sat by themselves at one of the long tables and looked at the fried cabbage in front of them.

"I should never have started liking it here!" said

Percy. "I knew it. It was a mistake. Now everything will be much worse. And now I've gone around liking it for a whole year."

That was how long he'd been living in Stureby. Before that Percy had lived in a lot of places where he put leaflets in letterboxes and his father sold Venetian blinds till no one wanted to buy them any more. Percy hadn't been very sad to move, because he'd never made any real friends. And the teachers didn't seem sorry to see him go either.

"But here it's been different," he said. "Here I have you, and you're almost my brother. I've had so much fun that I forgot we always have to move. And I've learned how to do addition."

"Yeah," said Ulf. "It's a bummer about the hypnosis. What else can we do?"

Percy had to think about that for a bit.

"I'll just have to stop liking it here," he said. "Otherwise I'll never be able to move."

He poked at his food.

Then he went and ripped off Charlie's cap and stamped on it.

"What're you doing?" said Charlie. "Have you gone crazy again? I thought we were friends now."

Percy didn't answer. He went out without saying a word.

"What's up with him?" Charlie asked when Ulf came up and dusted off his cap.

"Yeah, what did he go and do that for?" said Olle Rickberg.

"Don't you get it?" said Ulf. "He did it because he didn't want to."

"Ah ha, so that's it," said Charlie, scratching his ear.

"Yes," said Ulf. "It's because he has to move soon. So now we have to be nice to him."

When it was time to go home, everyone was nice to Percy.

Olle Rickberg asked him if he wanted to borrow his bicycle. Charlie said he could stamp on his cap again. Ulf suggested that they all went to his place to eat his mother's buns, and practice fainting.

But Percy just shook his head.

"It won't work," he said. "Because I'll just start liking it even more."

That afternoon Ulf, Olle Rickberg and Charlie played by themselves. They played the same way they had done for a long time before Percy came. They practised walking the tightrope on a clothesline they tied between two pine trees in the little woods at Olle Rickberg's house. They danced around under the sprinklers sweeping jets of water onto Charlie's lawn, till their clothes were dripping wet.

But even though they laughed as hard as they could and pretended that everything was just fine, it wasn't the same as it had been. Because even though Percy hadn't moved yet, they had already begun to miss him.

CHAPTER EIGHT

A sheik is coming to Stureby

In the days following, Percy did everything he could so that he would want to leave Stureby. He went off on his own to the forbidden oak tree at school. He ripped school caps off small children and tried to fall out with as many people as he could.

On Monday he hit his thumbs with the hammer at woodwork. On Tuesday when no one wanted to eat lunch because it was fish balls, he asked the ladies for the biggest portion they could give him.

Then he sat at the table and looked at the pale grey, jelly lumps.

"Geez," he said. "This has to be the most horrible food there is."

"Yes, I think it is," said Ulf.

Percy speared a fish ball on his fork and held it in front of his face. He pinched his nostrils together.

"Now!" he said.

He began to eat. It went slowly. It took the whole lunch time. Every mouthful he swallowed looked as if it was going to come back up. He was as pale grey as a fish ball himself by the time he'd finished.

"Now I'm going to ask for a second helping," he said.

He got halfway up. But Ulf pulled him down onto his chair again.

"Don't do it," he said. "You'll die of food poisoning."

"Yeah, maybe I will," said Percy. "I haven't ever felt as sick as this before."

He had to sit there for quarter of an hour, rocking back and forth and holding his stomach, before Ulf could lead him back to the classroom.

But all the way he smiled a very satisfied smile.

"Sheez," he giggled. "Sheez, I feel awful. I won't ever want to go back in there."

When they got to the classroom everyone was cleaning their desks out. They had to clean up all the bits of old rubber left over from rubbing out, put back the coloured crayons in their boxes, and put their books in nice tidy piles.

Percy didn't want to clean his desk, because if he did he would only think about how he had to move. So he sat by himself in the window seat instead.

He stood with his nose against the window pane,

trying to get air. He was looking at the schoolyard where he had played so many times. He looked at the field where he'd hit the ball so hard with the baseball bat that it disappeared into the bushes. And a long way away, behind Orby, was Munkfors which was something he didn't want to think about. Every now and then he sighed and felt his stomach.

After a while Berra put up his hand.

"Excuse me, aren't we supposed to be cleaning out our desks?" he asked.

"That's right," said the teacher.

"So why isn't Percy doing it then?" said Berra. "Is he allowed to just sit and look out the window?"

The teacher looked at Percy. She looked at the back of his neck.

"Yes," she said. "He can sit there as long as he likes."

That's when Percy broke the window. A cloud of small sharp bits of glass fell to the floor. The classroom went absolutely quiet. But the teacher was already there and she helped Percy down from the window seat.

"Oh dear, oh dear," she said. "Percy, what were you thinking?"

"I was thinking of Munkfors," said Percy.

The teacher didn't say anything. She gave him a hug and stroked his neck with her hand.

"Aren't you going to get angry now?" asked Percy.

"No," she said. "It was an accident. And accidents can happen to anybody."

Then Percy pulled away. He looked as if he would burst into tears any minute.

"Why do you all have to be so nice?" he yelled. "Why can't you scream and clip me round the ears instead? Any other teacher would have!"

Then he ran out through the door.

The teacher stood beside the broken window and watched him run across the yard holding his stomach.

That evening Ulf was sitting in his green room with the dogs on the walls. He didn't want to go out. He didn't even want to meet Marianne, even though she asked him if they could meet down by the field.

He wasn't in the mood for kissing.

He thought about his best friend Percy and about what he could do to help him, but he couldn't think of anything. So he did his homework instead and then it was time for his hot chocolate.

Normally his father was very strict about mealtimes. He wanted them all to eat together. That's because he had read in the book about bringing up children that eating together as a family is important. But today it was about twenty minutes before he came up from his radio apparatus. His hair was sticking out like angel wings and his face was as red as his tie.

"My dear family," he said. "This is a big day for us."

"Is it?" said Ulf's mother. "What's happened?"

"I have just talked to Prince Talal from Saudi Arabia," said Dad, kissing her on the cheek.

"That's lovely," she said. "What did he say?"

"He asked what sort of weather we're having," said Dad. "And I told him it was clear and warm."

"Well I never," said Ulf's mother. "Fancy a real prince asking about what kind of weather we're having."

"Didn't he say anything else?" Jan asked.

Ulf's Dad took a celebratory bite of his sandwich. He chewed it thoroughly and then he took a mouthful of hot chocolate, before he answered.

"Yes, he did, actually," he said after an eternity. "Can you guess what he said?"

"No, we can't," said Jan. "What did he say?"

"He said he was coming here," said Ulf's dad.

"Here to Sweden?" asked his mother.

"Here to Stureby, my dear," said Dad proudly. "Here to us on our street. He wants to meet a real live amateur radio enthusiast from Sweden."

"When is he coming?" asked Ulf's mother.

"Actually, I forgot to ask," said his Dad. "But anyway, I said that he could come here for dinner."

"Oh my goodness," said Ulf's mother. "What will we have?"

"We'll think of something," said Dad. "Brown beans and pork belly is pretty good."

"Yeah, and apple sauce," said Ulf.

His mother left to go to the toilet.

After a while Ulf left as well. He went up to his room again because Jan and his father were going to reset all the clocks in the house.

CHAPTER NINE

At last Percy starts to want to move

After school Percy joined Ulf and the others less and less often. He couldn't take the risk that they would do something fun, he said.

"But what about shooting the air gun? That's not so much fun," Ulf said one day.

"No, you're right," said Percy. "And I can always miss. I hate that."

So they all went together to Munksund Street to shoot targets with Bjorn's air gun: Percy, Charlie, Olle Rickberg and Ulf.

They passed the Corso cinema, the Medical Centre and the petrol station with the red MOBIL pump. They stopped outside the mechanic's workshop and looked at a broken-down Ford Anglia. And then they looked at a DKW with a ding on its front bumper.

"Do you know what DKW means," Percy asked.

"I think I know," said Charlie. "But I can't remember right now."

Percy giggled and said some very rude words.

They all laughed. Ulf did too, even though he didn't understand it. He laughed because Percy had made a joke. They all laughed so much they ran out of breath, till Percy caught sight of a Saab. Then he stopped laughing. He walked off so fast that Ulf had to half-run to keep up with him.

"What would you be doing if I wasn't here?" Percy asked after a while.

"I dunno," said Ulf. "Probably I would go to the cake shop with Marianne. She asked if we could."

"Do it then," said Percy.

"But I said we could do it another day," said Ulf. "I told her I'd rather be with you."

When they got to Munksund Street, Lasse was there with his back to the sun, shadow-boxing a plank. He was hopping around, boxing the air so hard it made his neck sweat.

"Hi Lasse," said Ulf. "How's your hand?"

Lasse turned to them. But he didn't say anything.

"Aren't you going to call us snot faces today?" asked Percy.

"Nah, I'm not going to," said Lasse.

"And you're not going to hit us either?" asked Percy.

"Do you think I'm stupid? Think I want to be hypnotised and get an egg on my skull?"

"So that means we can call you a numbskull then," said Percy.

"Whaddid you say?" said Lasse.

"I said you're a numbskull," giggled Percy. "A full-blown corkscrew. I've always wanted to say that."

Before Ulf could get hold of Percy, Lasse grabbed his checked shirt and shook him.

"Do you know what a hiding you'd get if Ulf couldn't do hypnosis?" he hissed.

"He can't do it any more," said Percy.

So Lasse hit him. He hit him so hard straight on the chin, that he fell over. Even when Ulf quickly counted to twenty and told Lasse that he was feeling more and more tired, nothing happened. Lasse just looked more pleased and started to punch Percy in the stomach.

"Ha ha!" he laughed. "You can't do hypnotising any more, Ulf! It's just like Percy said. Try something else on me, eh!"

"An Arabian sheik is coming to our house," said Ulf.

Lasse stopped fighting and stared at Ulf.

"You're lying again," he said. "Gee, I hate it when people lie straight to my face."

"I'm not lying. It's true," said Ulf. "I'll bet you anything you want."

"Okay then," said Lasse. "If he doesn't come I'll make you into jelly. And I'll have that gold watch you had when you hypnotised me."

"Nah, I dunno," said Ulf. "It's Dad's best one. It was made by a dead watchmaker from Russia."

"Then I'll keep on fighting," said Lasse and he raised his hand.

"No, don't," said Ulf. "But if the sheik comes you must never fight again. And not before either."

Lasse got up off Percy's legs. He brushed the dust off his trousers and held out his hand so they could press thumbs together.

It was the first time Ulf had pressed thumbs with a boxing glove.

When Lasse had wandered off, Ulf leant over Percy.

"How are you?" he asked.

"It hurts everywhere," mumbled Percy and got up off the ground.

"What did you have to say that for?" Ulf asked. "Why did you have to tell him that I can't do hypnosis any more?"

"To get myself a hiding," Percy smiled with bloody lips. "And it worked! Now I'm really starting to want to move."

There was no air gun shooting that afternoon, because Percy wanted to go home to start packing.

"Good that you came up with the thing about the sheik in any case," he said. "He's a real screw-top, Lasse is. But trust me, you'll regret it."

Ulf stayed and watched Percy limping off on his squashed legs.

That day Ulf had macaroni pudding with raspberry jam.

It had a hard black skin on top because his mother had forgotten to take it out of the oven. She had so much to think about these days. She had to change all the curtains. She had to dust all the skirtings, polish the chandelier and read the *Big Cookbook*. Now she was sitting, staring at the burnt dinner.

"It doesn't matter, dear," said Ulf's father, taking a big bite. "It's almost better like this. Isn't it, boys?"

"It doesn't matter what you say," she sighed. "A burned pudding is a burned pudding. And this is no food to give to royalty. Imagine if dinner's burnt when the prince comes."

"Ach, don't worry about that. When it comes down to it, maybe he won't come at all."

"He has to," said Ulf.

"You have to try and get hold of him in any case, Kurt," said his mother. "You must try and find out if and when he's coming."

"I know, I know," said Ulf's father.

No one said anything for a long time. You could hear Dad's back teeth grinding when he chewed. Ulf's mother pressed her fingers to her temples as if she was about to get a migraine. It felt so gloomy that Ulf wanted to cheer them all up.

"Do you want to hear a funny story?" he asked, after a while.

"Not a silly one," said Jan.

"No-no, this is really funny," said Ulf. "Everyone laughs when they hear it. Do you know what DKW means?"

"No, what can it mean?" said his mother. "Eskil has that sort of car."

Ulf repeated Percy's words.

He was told to leave the table.

Dad said he never wanted to hear words like that in his house again. Then he sent Ulf up to his room, and told him to stay there the rest of the day and to think about how stupid he'd been.

When it was almost dark Jan came in. Ulf had already put on his light-blue pyjamas and got into bed. Jan had an old comic. He was being nice this year.

"That was funny what you said at dinner," he said.

"Mum and Dad didn't think so," Ulf sighed.

"Nah," said Jan. "Why did you say it, you idiot?"

"I just wanted them to laugh," said Ulf. "I don't even know what it means. What does it mean?"

"Nah," said Jan. "I'll tell you when you're older."

Then he sat down on the edge of the bed and talked about Saudi Arabia instead. He talked about sheiks who were so rich that they could buy anything they wanted. They had at least twenty wives and flashy big American cars with built-in fridges, cars so long that they almost couldn't go round corners. Then he said that if you asked an Arabian sheik for something, he had to give it to you straight away.

"That's not true," said Ulf.

"It is, it's dead true," said Jan.

"Who said so?" asked Ulf.

"Dad said so," said Jan. "He said so when we were fixing a switch. But now you need to go to sleep. Good night!"

"Good night," said Ulf.

He put his head on the pillow and shut his eyes. He could hear his mother playing the piano and singing downstairs.

"*Getting better all the time*," she sang with her wobbly voice, and Ulf went to sleep smiling.

He dreamed about American cars driving around in the desert and lots of other things, then in the middle of the night he found his brother shaking him awake.

"Hello, wake up!" he said. "Are you having a nightmare?"

"No, I don't think so," said Ulf, blinking.

"It sounded like you were," said Jan.

"How did it sound?" asked Ulf.

"Woof, woof," said his brother.

CHAPTER TEN

Three princess cakes and a surprise

Everyone knew by now that Ulf had lied and that he couldn't do hypnosis at all. Bengt wanted his Roy Rogers film card back again. Berra said that he'd known all along that it was rubbish.

"And do you know what he's saying now?" he giggled. "He says an Arabian sheik is coming to visit!"

Everybody laughed. They laughed until Percy told them to shut up and go into the classroom. He followed to make sure they really went. Then Marianne came up to Ulf.

"Don't worry about them," she said. "I know you were not lying. Can you go to the cake shop with me today?"

"Yes, I probably can," said Ulf, "because Percy is going home to start packing."

"Shall we say three o'clock at the corner bakery then?" asked Marianne.

"Sure," said Ulf. "That sounds good."

Marianne went on her way. But when she got to the flag pole she turned around and gave him such a smile that her front teeth shone in the sun.

"You'll get a surprise, anyhow!" she called out. "It's about that thing you hypnotised me to do in the woods!"

The last class was gymnastics. Ulf and Percy went behind a box horse, because everyone was going to walk the beam and that was one of Percy's favourite things. They sat with their backs against the box and listened to the sound of Bengt falling to the floor and the teacher blowing her metal whistle.

"Are you doing anything special after school?" whispered Ulf.

"Yes, I'm helping Dad take down the curtain rails," said Percy. "We don't have much time left, you know."

"Shame," said Ulf. "Otherwise you could have come with me to the corner shop bakery. I'm meeting Marianne."

"Sounds fun," mumbled Percy.

"Yeah," said Ulf. "Will you come then?"

"Nah," said Percy. "I don't want to have fun. And anyway it's better if we get used to not being together."

"I don't want to," said Ulf.

"You'll still have Marianne," muttered Percy just as the bell rang and everyone rushed towards the changing room.

Only Percy wasn't in a hurry.

He was still sitting behind the box.

As Ulf walked alongside the hedge by the old people's home he could taste the toothpaste he had used called DENTOSAL. It was nasty toothpaste that tasted mostly of salt. His father had at least a thousand free tubes of it. Ulf had his wallet in his back pocket. And he had washed under his arms and combed his hair with hair cream.

Now he was ready to go to the cake shop. The clock at the train station said quarter to three when he turned left and went past the empty rugby field. Then all he had to do was go straight up the street and he was there.

Marianne was already there waiting.

The cake shop's red neon letters glowed above her blond hair. She was wearing a skirt, a belt and a fluffy Angora jumper. She was also looking freshly-combed and beautiful.

"Hi Ulf," she said. "Shall we go in?"

"Ye-es," he said.

Marianne took him by the hand up to the counter that was full with lovely cakes and buns. A lady with blue hair and a white apron stood on the other side.

"What will it be today?" she asked, looking at Marianne.

Ulf turned to Marianne and took out his wallet.

"Choose whatever you like," he said. "I'll pay."

Marianne took a long time to choose. She looked at the bright green cakes, the Schwarzwaldt cakes sprinkled with lovely chocolate flakes and the fluffy cream buns with small, shiny pieces of fruit on them.

"Well, I don't know," she said finally. "But those ones look very good."

"Then we'll have two of those," said Ulf to the shop lady.

"Could we make it three?" said Marianne.

They sat down at a window table with a flower pot on it, and enjoyed the delicious taste of the buns. Ulf took tiny little bites of his bun to make the moment last forever. And Marianne seemed to be thinking the same thing, because she just sipped the red fizzy Ulf had ordered, and picked a little at one of her buns.

Now and then she looked out through the window. Ulf thought he should come up with something clever to say so she wouldn't think he was any old idiot.

"Very good buns," he said at last.

She turned from the window and looked him in the eyes. Her cheeks were as red as the fizzy bubbling in their glasses.

"Oh, I'm so happy," she said.

"Me too," said Ulf.

"I'm happy because I met you," she said. "Do you remember what you hypnotised me to do last time?"

"Yes, I remember," he said. "I said that you would fall in love with a boy with blond hair, chubby cheeks and quite fat thighs."

"That's right," she said. "And you were right. I'm in love."

Ulf forgot that he wanted a dog. He squeezed Marianne's hand beside the flower pot and his eyes felt warm with happiness. He licked the cream from his lips and bent closer to her mouth. Then suddenly she stretched out her other hand.

"It's him," she whispered.

"What?" said Ulf.

"That's who I'm in love with!" Marianne said and she pointed to the boy who had just come in.

He had blond hair and chubby cheeks. A pair of thighs much fatter than Ulf's stuck out from under his shorts.

"Isn't he cute?" asked Marianne. "His name is Arne. He has a poodle we take for walks. I just wanted you to meet him somehow."

"Nice," said Ulf.

Then Arne squeezed his thighs in under their table. And Marianne pushed the saucer with the untouched bun towards him.

"Here you are," she said. "It was Ulf's shout."

When Ulf got home his mother was cleaning the oven. She had polished the piano till it shone in the afternoon sun, and she had rolled up all the rugs and carried them out onto the terrace.

"I thought you could help me beat them," she said. "Then I can get on with cleaning the windows."

"I can do that," Ulf said.

He was thinking that it was nice not to be alone. His mother stood behind him, cleaning the windows so hard they squeaked. He hit the rugs with the bamboo whisk. He liked the sound it made and he hit them as hard as he could. All the time he was thinking of Arne.

He thought about his fat thighs and about how unfair it was that Arne had a dog and about Marianne's shining smile when she talked to him.

"My, you're giving them a hard time today!" called his mother.

"So they'll be nice for when the sheik comes," said Ulf, wiping his eyes because of the dust.

His mother stopped rubbing the windows.

"He's not coming," she said. "Your father talked to him yesterday. He said that unfortunately he won't have time to visit us when he comes to Sweden."

"Why not?" asked Ulf.

"I don't know why not," his mother said. "I suppose he will be meeting the king."

"Why are we doing all this cleaning then?" asked Ulf.

"It's become a habit," said his mother.

They didn't say much after that. His mother kept cleaning the windows. Ulf carried on beating the rugs, though he wasn't hitting them as hard now, because he was thinking about Lasse and that was enough to make anyone lose the strength in their arms.

"Do you know what?" said his mother when they were finished. "I think it's quite good that he's not coming, that sheik. But don't say anything to your father, because he is very, very disappointed."

They went into the kitchen to make meat balls together.

As Ulf rolled meat balls in the kitchen he thought about his disappointed father. He knew himself how it felt to be disappointed.

"He really wanted to meet a sheik, didn't he?" he said.

"Yes," his mother said. "It would have given him a lot of pleasure. But he will get over it, if we give him a bit of TLC."

"Of course," said Ulf.

Then he said he was going upstairs to wash his hands.

On the way to the attic he sneaked into his parents' bedroom. He took the powder that his mother put on her face when she didn't want to look so pale. Then he took the pen she used for painting her eyebrows.

He was quite a long time in the bathroom. He knew what his father was like when he was disappointed. He would go round with great sorrowful eyes. Sometimes he wouldn't say a word for a week.

He was only just satisfied by the time his mother called the third time for him to come down and eat. He put on the too-big dressing gown Granddad had given him for Christmas. He had tied a towel on his head with the dressing gown belt. His face looked sunburned, and he had a beard and a moustache.

"Good evening," Ulf said as he entered the dining room, with a voice as deep as he could manage. "I have come directly from Arabia. I have come to visit you."

"What?" said his father and looked up from his jam.

"I think I have arrived in time for dinner?" rumbled Ulf. "Fantastic! And this is dentist Stark, I believe?"

He took a step towards his father who was staring at

his brown powdered face, at the dressing gown and the towel on his head. Then his father pushed back his chair and half got up.

"Don't get up," said Ulf. "Don't let me disturb you."

His father pointed at the door.

"Leave the room, Ulf," he said. "Go upstairs immediately and take off all that stuff. And never put it on again."

So Ulf left the room. But in the doorway he turned around.

"I was only trying to be kind," he said. "I only wanted you to see a sheik for once in your life."

CHAPTER ELEVEN

Jan is nice and throws Ulf into the piano

One Thursday when Percy came to school, they almost didn't recognise him. He was wearing a white shirt and a big red tie with white spots that he had borrowed from his father. He had combed his hair and his backpack looked heavy and knobbly.

"You are looking very nice today," said the teacher. "Are you going to a party after school?"

"No," he said.

And he sat down in his chair.

He sat quietly all through writing and geography. He didn't say anything until school was almost finished and the teacher was talking about Jesus. She was talking about the time he gathered all his disciples together so they could say farewell and eat dinner together for the last time.

Percy stood up beside his chair.

"Excuse me," he said, "but there's something I'd like to say."

"And what would that be?" said the teacher.

"Goodbye," he said.

"What?" she said. "Are you leaving already?"

"No, I'm moving," he said. "I am going to live in Munkfors and I'll never be coming back."

Then the teacher looked at his tie and his white shirt and you could see she didn't know what to say.

"But my dear child," she said. "Are you leaving straight away?"

"No, in two weeks," said Percy. "But I thought I might not manage to say it later."

So he went round to everybody one by one.

"Goodbye, Charlie," he said. "Goodbye, Olle Rickberg!"

He shook everyone by the hand and made a little bow.

When at last he got to Ulf he put out his hand, then he took it back again.

"We'll say goodbye later," he said. "Now I'm going to say goodbye to the teacher."

He rummaged in his tattered backpack and took out a parcel with a ribbon rosette on its top corner. Then he went and placed it on the desk in front of the teacher.

"I'm giving you this because you've been so nice," he said. "All my other teachers have been shitty."

The teacher looked as if she needed to wipe her eyes on his tie. She took a long time to open the parcel, but finally she did. Inside was an apparatus with a plastic pink hood and a piece of rubber hose attached.

The teacher hugged Percy hard.

"Thank you, Percy dear," she said. "But what on earth is it for?"

"It's a potato peeling machine," said Percy. "It kind of got left out when we were packing. Do you like it?"

"I like it a lot," she said.

"I thought it would be the thing for you," said Percy, pleased. "Then you can think about me when you peel the potatoes."

The teacher put down the potato peeler and hugged him again.

"There's no chance that I'll ever forget you," she said.

"The teacher seemed to like the potato thing," Percy said as he and Ulf went down the hill towards the post office.

"Yeah, you could see that," said Ulf.

"Piece of luck," said Percy. "Mum didn't like it. Dad gave it to her for Christmas. But she thought it made too much noise."

"Yeah, it's hard to know what girls like," said Ulf.

"But you like ice cream, I know that," said Percy.

And he took Ulf to the green ice cream shop and he bought two cones called Top Hat which is the biggest and nicest ice cream there is. Then they stood in the sun and ate their ice cream in silence. It was almost like when Jesus and the disciples ate their dinner together for the last time.

"Well," said Percy when they had finished. "That's it then. Thursday after next I'll be a long way away from here."

They looked at each other. They knew they wouldn't see each other any more after school.

"Thanks for the ice cream," said Ulf.

Then they turned for home.

Suddenly Lasse Agren popped up behind the shop. He was bright red in the face and he waved his right-hand glove at Ulf.

"Hey, I've been looking all over for you," he puffed. "You tricked me anyway. There is no sheik. So now you have to be punished. And I'm going to get that gold watch!"

"Don't be stupid," said Percy. "Of course he's coming. It just got a bit complicated with his private jet planes."

"That's right," said Ulf.

Lasse looked from one to the other.

"I still think you're lying," he said. "But he has to

come before Monday in two weeks' time. Because that's when I have the right-hand glove again."

"Saturday at the earliest," said Percy.

"Tuesday," said Lasse.

"Okay, then we'll make it Wednesday," said Percy.

Lasse nodded. Then he went on his way. Percy thrust his hands into his pockets and went off without looking back a single time. Ulf stood and watched his friend going up the hill. He got smaller and smaller, till he was just a little thing with downcast shoulders.

"One day you'll be a great businessman!" Ulf called after him. "One day you'll do the deal of your life!"

Ulf's dad sat alone at his desk, staring at the shining globe. Every now and again he would sigh. And every now and then he would turn the globe as if he was hoping to sight a private jet somewhere over the shining blue sea.

Voices were crackling from the radio when Ulf went down to him with a cup of calming herbal tea his mother had made.

"You haven't heard any more from him?" asked Ulf.

"Who?" muttered his father.

"The sheik," said Ulf. "He hasn't said that he is going to come anyway?"

"No, Ulf," said his father. "And quite honestly I don't give a toss. I don't mind a bit."

"So he's not coming then?" asked Ulf.

"We will not talk about it any more," grumbled his father. "We won't ever talk about him again. Go up and play with Jan!"

So Ulf went. He went past the open fire. He looked at his father's expensive watch shining on the marble mantelpiece. And he wondered what his father would say when it disappeared and what Lasse was going to do Wednesday after next.

Then he went upstairs to his brother who was sitting peacefully in the flowery armchair in the living room, reading the latest edition of *House and Garden*.

"Can you teach me some ju-jitsu?" he asked.

"What for?" said Jan.

"In case I get attacked by some great oaf with boxing gloves, for example," said Ulf.

Jan got up, even though he hadn't finished reading.

"We can practice on the rug by the piano," he said.

Jan was expert at tricky holds which made your arms feel as if they were about to fall off. He could dig with his fingers till you shrieked and wanted to give up straight away. And he knew how to push people's legs so they would fly onto their backsides.

"You make use of their strength," he said. "That's the

basic principle. That's what you have to learn. The stronger the other person is, the worse it'll be for him!"

"Good," said Ulf. "Because this one is very strong. Show me what to do if he tries to punch me in the nose."

So Jan did. He explained that you should grab hold of the other person's hand and twist it, at the same time making a half turn. Then you just had to bend your back and pull the arm, and the other person would fly off like a ghost.

"Got it?" said Jan.

"Sure," said Ulf.

But no matter how much he tried, he couldn't grab hold of Jan's hand. Time after time it stopped a millimetre short of his trembling nose.

"You're too slow, Ulf," said Jan. "I'll show you. Give me a right hander to the nose!"

"Promise you won't get mad if I hit you?" said Ulf.

"Promise," said Jan. "Show me your best punch!"

Ulf hesitated another second. He could hear his mother humming in the kitchen as she cleaned the silver. "*I'm longing for Italy*," she sang. Then he punched. He punched from underneath, just like when he did underarm girl's shots at baseball.

He got Jan right in the nose. When he pulled his hand back he could see Jan bending over the Persian rug.

"Sorry," he said.

"What the hell were you doing, you little louse!" yelled Jan.

"You promised you wouldn't get angry," said Ulf.

"I'm not angry," roared Jan. "But I said you should give me a right hander. And that was an upper cut."

"I didn't know that," said Ulf.

"You don't know anything," Jan sniffed, rubbing his red nose. "But you should never give up. Now try again. But remember – a right hander!"

So Ulf shot out his right fist.

And this time Jan grabbed hold of his wrist.

In half a second he had twisted his arm and bent his back so that Ulf flew across the room.

There was a powerful, thundering sound as he landed on the piano.

"Something like that," said Jan. "Have you got it now?"

Ulf just shook his head. His mother came rushing in from the kitchen with a newly polished silver spoon in her hand.

"What in heaven's name are you up to, boys?" she shouted. "I don't understand what has got into you. You know your father needs peace and quiet."

Then she caught sight of Ulf lying stretched out on the floor with his feet under the piano stool.

"Oh my goodness," she said. "What has Jan done? He hit you."

"Nah, Jan was being nice," said Ulf. "He was just trying to teach me something I am never going to learn in my whole life."

He was still lying on the floor when Jan and his mother went out. He lay with his head pointing towards the Persian rug, thinking about Lasse and Marianne and Percy. And about how life could be so wonderful and so sorrowful.

CHAPTER TWELVE

Ulf visits Percy's father

The Friday before he was going to move, Percy cried in the middle of art. The teacher had said they should draw something nice that they remembered from summer.

Ulf drew a dog, because he was good at them. He drew a Gordon setter, lifting its nose to the sky. He had just finished the tail when he heard Percy sniff. When he turned around, he saw tears pouring down Percy's cheeks and falling onto his drawing paper.

The whole classroom went quiet, because no one had ever seen Percy cry. Some of them would cry at the smallest thing, if they fell over in the schoolyard and grazed their knees or if they got their fingers caught in the door. But Percy wasn't one of them. He wasn't the sort to cry.

"But dear child, what's the matter?" asked the teacher when she came to his desk.

"Ach," Percy sniffled. "I was just thinking about all the fun things I did in the summer."

"Ah-ha," said the teacher, and held up his drawing.

It was a picture of two naked ladies sunbathing in the grass. They were the assistants at the old people's home that Ulf and his friends had spied on from the roof of Olle Rickberg's tool shed.

"Yes, you seem to have been quite busy," said the teacher and put the drawing back on the desk.

"Now it's all over," said Percy.

He folded the paper up carefully and put it in his pocket. Then he dried his cheeks with his shirt sleeve.

"Is that better now?" asked the teacher. "How do you feel?"

"Like shit," said Percy and he left the room without even closing the door.

The teacher went back to her desk. She sat down and stared helplessly at the map of Scandinavia hanging on the wall.

"Did you hear what Percy said?" asked Berra.

"He swore," said the teacher. "And I want to, too. And now you can all finish what you've been doing."

That day Ulf didn't go home for afternoon tea. He went wandering round the streets. He looked at the pear tree where the pears would soon be ripe. And he looked at the chestnut tree which was full of green and prickly balls.

But it didn't make him feel happy.

Because what was good about picking pears at dusk if you weren't with your best friend?

Slowly he wound his way back along the street.

At Nilvert's hardware store he bumped into Marianne who had been to buy fish in the fish shop with the running glass window.

"Hello," he said. "Aren't you with Arne?"

"No, he is practising playing the washboard this evening," she said. "Would you like to walk home with me a bit of the way?"

"Not today," said Ulf. "I'm going to Percy's house. But there's something I want to ask you first."

"What's that?" she asked.

"Can't you go around with Arne and me?" said Ulf. "In Saudi Arabia you can be married to at least twenty people at once. And it works out really well."

"Not for me," said Marianne. "I can only be in love with one man at a time."

"Shame," said Ulf. "I thought I might as well ask. Now I have to go."

"See you," said Marianne.

Ulf could still smell fish when he went off towards Percy's place.

Percy's father opened the door when Ulf rang the bell. He was wearing the same nylon shirt as the last time, but today he looked even more tired.

"So it's you, Ulf," he said. "Percy's not home. He's gone out to find more empty packing boxes."

"It doesn't matter," said Ulf. "It was you I wanted to see anyway."

"Is that right?" said Percy's father. "Well, please won't you come in then."

They went through the hall. There was a single lamp shining from the ceiling and the walls were lined with suitcases and cartons. Only the hall mirror hung where it usually did.

"Please excuse the mess," said Percy's father. And he sat down in the sofa and crossed his legs.

"Now," he said. "What's on your mind?"

Ulf looked at Percy's father's black shoe which was bobbing up and down. It felt strange looking at it. And it was scary to be in a room where all the rugs were rolled up against the walls, and where there weren't any curtains left. It made him feel sad and angry at the same time.

"So, Ulf," said Percy's father. "Tell me what you came to say."

"I just wanted to tell you that you shouldn't move," said Ulf.

"Yes, yes I know," said Percy's father, looking at the wall.

"Percy's really sad," said Ulf. "Me too. Don't you know that?"

"Is there anything else you wanted to say?" said Percy's father.

"Yes," said Ulf. "Percy wants to go on living here. It's actually the only place he's ever been really happy. He never asked to move."

"No," said Percy's father.

"Today he even started crying in the middle of drawing," said Ulf. "It looks like you're only bloody well thinking of yourself!"

"Is that what you think?" said Percy's father.

Ulf just nodded, because suddenly all the anger and words inside him had dried up. For a moment there was absolute silence in the room. Percy's father stopped jiggling his foot. He wiped his hand over his eyes.

"You shouldn't swear, Ulf," he said. "Sometimes it feels as if you have to. But you should always fight it."

"Yes," said Ulf.

"Now listen to me," he said. "Your father is a dentist. People come to him and get the holes in their teeth fixed. Some of them need false teeth and others want gold teeth. Is that right?"

"Yes," said Ulf.

"And all the time people keep getting new holes in their teeth," said Percy's father. "And that means your father gets more money. Dentists don't have to worry about whether there is enough money. They have enough to manage. But it's not like that for everybody. Have you never thought of that?"

"No-o," said Ulf. "No, I never have."

"You think I'm only thinking of myself," he went on. "You think I don't know that Percy wants to stay here. Actually there's nothing I want more. You don't think I want my wife to be able to buy herself a lambskin coat even though it's still summer? I sell Venetian blinds, Ulf. And if no one wants to buy my Venetian blinds we have to move. What else can I do?"

"I don't know," said Ulf.

Suddenly he understood. He understood that he couldn't do anything to help Percy, and that Percy's father couldn't do anything either.

"Not all fathers have money sitting in the bottom of the chest," said Percy's father.

"No, mine has his in the Nordic family book," said Ulf.

Percy's father got up.

"I'm sorry, Ulf," he said. "I'm sorry that everything is the way it is. But I'm still pleased that you came here. And I'm glad that Percy has you as his best friend."

When Ulf went out Percy's mother was standing in the middle of all the boxes in the hall. She was wearing her new lambskin coat. She was standing unmoving in front of the mirror, and she looked happy, as if she was dreaming that she was somewhere completely different.

The street lamps were already lit when Ulf got home. And so was the idiotic sign which said: Reg. Dentist Kurt Stark.

"Do you have any idea how many hours late you are for dinner?" said Ulf's father when he came inside.

"No-o," said Ulf.

"Three-and-a-half," said Ulf's father, looking at the clock in the hall.

"Oh," said Ulf.

"But what does it matter?" said Ulf's father. "Because today is a wonderful day. Today I have received a luxury telegram from prince Talal Al Saud of Saudi Arabia. And he writes that he would like to come and visit after all."

"When is he coming?" said Ulf.

"On Wednesday," said his father. "And now I'll come with you upstairs to the kitchen and heat up your stew."

"Will you?" said Ulf.

"Yes," said his father. "Your mother has a little headache. So she is in the bedroom having a rest."

Ulf had never seen his dad do anything in the kitchen before. But now there he was, stirring the pot with a wooden spoon, whistling happily under the newly-washed oven hood.

Ulf sat at the kitchen table tasting the stew his father had managed to make look like dog food.

"You know Dad," he said. "Is it true that you can have anything you want if you ask an Arabian sheik? Jan said you said so."

"No," said his father, wrinkling his forehead. "It's just something I heard. But I have also heard that to ask is the most impolite thing you can ever do. If you do you can end up in disgrace forever. Do you not want any more dinner?"

"No, I'm not so hungry," said Ulf.

CHAPTER THIRTEEN

Potato dumplings and ice hockey

The night before the sheik's visit Ulf's mother was not herself. The last few days she had been on the go from morning to late at night. She had combed the fringes on the Persian rugs with a steel comb. She had rubbed the cupboard doors with Phenomenon and baked so that the cookie jar was full of coconut balls. And she had ironed all the table cloths at least twice.

Now she was sitting in the bedroom when Ulf came in.

She was sitting in front of the mirror in her red evening dress, looking at herself with a frown between her eyes. She had her black hair loose so that it hung all the way down her back.

"Is there anything I can help you with?" asked Ulf.

"No, no," she said. "I just want some peace for a moment!"

And she picked up a pair of scissors from the bedroom table.

Ulf ran downstairs where Jan and his father were on their knees trying out the new electric fire that Ulf's father had bought.

"Hurry! Hurry!" he shouted. "Mum's cutting off her hair!"

That put some speed into Ulf's father, because he loved his wife's long, black hair that she hadn't cut since she was twelve. He ran the whole way up to the bedroom.

"What in heaven's name are you doing?" he said puffing in the doorway.

Ulf's mother put down the scissors.

"I look like nothing on earth," she said. "I'm fat. I have wrinkles round my eyes. Not to mention the hair. I can't have all this with a prince coming."

"Don't touch your hair!" said Ulf's father. "I'd rather ring the Grand Hotel and tell him not to come."

Ulf and Jan were standing in the doorway and they saw how their father gently stroked their mother's shoulders, beneath the red dress with the lace on it.

"Come on Ulf," said Jan. "Let's get out of here."

So they did.

Jan went up to his room to try on his new tie. Ulf rang Lasse Agren from the telephone in the dental rooms.

"I wasn't lying," he said. "He's coming to dinner tomorrow. You can probably see him driving up the street in his flash American car."

"Who's that?" said Lasse.

"The sheik," said Ulf. "The sheik from Arabia."

Ulf had been waiting at least two hours at the window beside the Christmas cactus when a big, open-topped car pulled up. It was a Cadillac. It was white with long tail wings and chrome edgings which shone in the sun. It parked by their mail box.

Behind it was a DKW with Eskil and the engineer Carl Johan Abom. They were his father's amateur radio friends.

"Hello! Hello!" called Ulf. "They're here already!"

"Oh my goodness," said his mother. "And I haven't finished the butter balls yet. Dad will have to take care of them! I think I'll go and hide up in the attic."

Ulf's father opened the door.

And there was a sheik, standing on the concrete step. He had a white cloth on his head. He was wearing a cloak made of thick black material. When Ulf took his hand he didn't squeeze, like most grown ups do. He just lay his hand in Ulf's. It was warm because it came from the desert.

"It is very kind of you to invite me here," he said.

He said it in a foreign language. But Ulf understood anyway, because the prince had an interpreter with him who translated everything he said.

"Maybe we can start by looking at the house?" Ulf's father suggested.

That's what he always said when guests arrived. He wanted to show them the house. He started by taking the sheik, the interpreter, Eskil and Mr Abom down to the basement. Ulf and Jan followed them.

"This, your Royal Highness, is the boiler," said Ulf's father, pointing. "And here we have the oil tank."

The Arabian prince nodded and looked politely at the pipes and at the big metal tank with oil in it. He sniffed the air in the basement as if he didn't want to miss any of it.

"The actual oil comes from Arabia," said Ulf.

The sheik smiled. But Jan pinched him in the arm.

"Keep your mouth shut!" he hissed.

"We'll move on then," said Ulf's father.

They went to the laundry and the pantry and the room where they kept rakes and spades and Ulf's father's moped called an ILO.

"This is my moped," he explained.

They continued to the attic, the living room and the library where the electric fire was on full blast. Ulf's father pointed proudly at everything. And the prince nodded. But he was starting to look tired.

"Very interesting," he said.

"Yes, now we only have the rumpus room remaining," said Ulf's father. "Then we can look at the radio apparatus."

On the table in the rumpus room there was the ice hockey game that Ulf and Jan played.

It was called a STIGA. It had players made of tin with yellow and red jerseys. The sheik stood in front of it and pulled the levers. For the first time he looked interested.

"And what is this, if I may ask?" he asked.

"It's table hockey," said Ulf

"I would very much like to try it," said the prince.

"We can play a game after dinner," said Ulf.

Because just then Ulf's mother had called out that dinner was ready.

Jan sulked the whole way through dinner. He was cross because Ulf was going to play hockey with the prince, even though Jan was the oldest.

"You can't even play properly for crissakes," he said as they carried the entrée plates back into the kitchen. "You will put the whole COUNTRY to shame!"

He pulled out Ulf's new bow tie, then let it ping into his neck.

"Stop it, boys," their mother hissed. "That's enough for today! It's bad enough that the sheik doesn't want to eat up all his dinner!"

She looked at the remains of the steak and horseradish sauce roll the prince had left on his plate. She took a deep breath and carried in the dish of potato dumplings.

Ulf's father loved potato dumplings. Once he had a competition with Grandpa and ate twenty-one. Jan's personal best was ten. But Ulf only ever managed three.

He didn't like the texture of them.

"This is real Swedish food," said Mr Abom.

"Very good," said the prince.

That, in any case, is what the interpreter said that he said. Still, the sheik ate only two dumplings. He took a single bite of the third and he picked out the small bits of pork and put them on the side.

Ulf's mother was crushed.

"He leaves everything," she whispered to the interpreter. "What shall I do? Shall I make a farmer's omelette?"

The interpreter smiled.

He said that everyone leaves food on their plates in Saudi Arabia, so that people can see they have had enough. Eating up everything on your plate would not be polite at all.

Ulf decided that he would also be polite.

Then Eskil, Mr Abom, Ulf's mother and father and Jan all understood that they should stop eating too.

Ulf's father looked hungrily at the steaming dumplings in front of him. He was very gloomy. He had only managed five.

"Ah well," he said. "We can have coffee later. Let's go down now and try out the radio apparatus."

"Yes, but first we're going to play some ice hockey," said Ulf.

"Yes, that would be very entertaining," said the sheik.

When Ulf got up he looked over at the veranda window. Lasse was there with wide eyes and his nose pressed against the window pane.

The sheik got to choose his team because he was the visitor. He chose the ones with the yellow jerseys, but it didn't matter. Ulf was used to having to be Russia. He had to be Russia every time he played with Jan.

They played 'First to Ten', three rounds, changing sides in between.

Ulf won the first round ten to five. The sheik couldn't find the right levers. And every time he tried to pass to the centre, Ulf's backs intercepted him.

But after they had changed sides he started to get the hang of it.

He got a goal straight away. It pinged into Ulf's goal net before Ulf had even got his hand on the goalie lever.

"Nice shot!" called Jan. He was supporting Saudi Arabia.

The sheik looked pleased when Ulf had to fish his puck out of the net.

"A most enjoyable game," he said. "Very exciting."

"Ye-es," said Ulf's father, even though he had never even tried to play it.

Mr Abom took care of the drop-in. He dropped the puck on the sheik's side every time. Ulf didn't complain, because he knew that if he did Jan would take off his centre for three minutes for "talking back at the umpire". That's what he usually did. And Jan was always the umpire.

The sheik won the second round ten to eight.

"Ulf doesn't have a chance," said the umpire.

And he was right. The sheik outclassed Ulf by ten to two in the last round. But what did it matter? Ulf was used to losing.

"Bravo, Your Highness," said Mr Abom. "Very nicely played."

"Ulf played well, too," said Eskil.

"Yes he did," smiled the sheik. "He has fulfilled my desire to play. He has given me a moment of the greatest excitement. Now I wonder if there is anything I can give him in return?"

Ulf couldn't believe his ears. And he didn't worry at all about the way his father was wrinkling his forehead.

"Yes," he said. "Actually there is something!"

"What is it that you desire, my friend?" asked the prince.

Ulf thought about the Newfoundland puppy with the blue-black coat. He thought about an Alsatian he could take out for a pee in the evening, or a yellow and white and black collie.

He cleared his throat.

"I would like to go and visit my friend Percy," he said. "His father sells Venetian blinds. But now he has to move, and I want him to meet a real sheik before he goes."

CHAPTER FOURTEEN

Percy does the deal of his life

Only Ulf, the sheik and the interpreter went to Percy's house. Mr Abom, Eskil and Ulf's father stayed and played with the radio equipment. His mother did the dishes. Jan was cross and said he would be in his room.

"We'll be back soon," said the sheik. "Ulf and I are just going on a little tour."

When they got to the car Lasse was waiting. His round face was long. He hung his head till he almost hit his nose on the metal letter box.

"You see," said Ulf. "I was telling the truth. And now we're going in the car to visit Percy."

"Wow," said Lasse. "Can I come too?"

"No," said Ulf. "There's no room."

They sat in the car. Ulf and the sheik sat in the back seat. The interpreter sat in the front, because he was going to drive.

"Just tell me where to turn," he said.

"Yes," said Ulf.

When the car glided off Lasse ran after it for quite a way. Ulf could see him getting smaller and smaller in the rear vision mirror. It felt good. The soft leather seats were also nice. He leaned back. And the sheik leaned back too.

"Personally I love to ride in the car," he said.

"I do too," said Ulf.

"Now you will see some fun," said the sheik.

He pushed a button. A hood miraculously came up over their heads. And when the sheik pushed the button again, it went down.

"Isn't that wonderful?" said the sheik.

"Yeeees," said Ulf.

As they drove past all the houses along the way, people opened their windows for a better look. Mr Gustavsson came out to polish his car. Mrs Ohlson was hanging out her washing as close to the street as she could get. Mrs Anderson stood with her hand in the letter box and curtsied as the car drove past, because a sheik had never before come to Stureby.

"Turn right here!" said Ulf when they got to the end of the street.

"Yes, and a bit faster, please if you don't mind!" said the sheik.

Then there were only a few more turns and they arrived at the house where Percy lived.

Ulf rang the doorbell. He rang two short and one long ring. That means 'U' in Morse code. Ulf had learned it from his father. So Percy would know that it was him.

But Percy didn't open the door. He talked through the letter box.

"We're not supposed to see each other any more," he said. "We've already said goodbye."

"I know," said Ulf. "But I have someone with me I want you to meet."

Percy opened the door. And he looked at the sheik, who looked back at him with his childlike, brown eyes.

"So this is Ulf's friend?" said the sheik. "It is a pleasure to meet you."

He stretched out his hand. Percy shook it thoroughly.

"It is a pleasure to meet you too," he said. "Please do come in."

They stepped into the hall.

"I thought you might like to ride in his car," whispered Ulf. "It's got a hood."

"Sure," said Percy. "But first I have to give him something."

His mother and father didn't even notice when they went past. They were in the living room doing the last of the packing. His mother was still wearing the lambskin coat. She was dancing around with a cushion in her arms, with Frank Sinatra singing on the gramophone. Percy's father wasn't even worrying about it. Normally he hated Frank Sinatra.

"*Don't worry 'bout me*," sang Frank Sinatra.

"Come on, let's go into my room," said Percy.

The interpreter and Ulf had to sit on the bed. The sheik sat in the guest chair at the desk. Percy stayed standing in the doorway.

"What can I get you?" he asked. "We have beer and Fanta."

"A Fanta would be good," said the sheik.

While Percy was out of the room, the sheik got up. He went over to the window. He was standing there when Percy came back with a tray with four bottles and straws.

They drank their Fantas and then they were quiet for a moment. When the sheik had drunk half his Fanta he put the bottle down on the window sill.

"A very good and thirst-quenching drink," he said.

"Yes," said Ulf. "Shall we go for a drive now?"

But the sheik had just discovered the lever for the Venetian blind that was still hanging in Percy's room.

He turned it and pulled it as if it was the manoeuvring lever for a game of hockey.

"What is this?" he asked.

Percy was only too happy to show him. He was at the window in a flash. He unwound the string from the button on the window edge so the blind fell down over the window.

"This is a Venetian blind, Mr Sheik," he said. "Go ahead and turn the lever!"

The sheik turned the lever. He saw how the thin metal bands opened and closed. He didn't want to stop. The whole time he was smiling like a happy child.

"A truly wonderful invention," he said.

"That's right," said Percy. "You just set them the way you want. Then you can have exactly as much or as little sun or shade as you like."

"I understand," said the sheik.

"It means people can't see in," said Percy. "And with just a simple hand movement you can pull it up again so the window is uncovered."

The sheik pulled the string and made the Venetian blind go up and down. Then he waved to the interpreter and said he should have a go, too.

"Very useful," said the sheik.

"Yes," said Percy. "Especially in places where there is a lot of sun. They are made from rust-proof material.

All you need to do is to wipe them with a damp cloth when they get dusty."

The sheik turned the lever a little.

"I come from a very sunny place," he said. "It is very nice to have shade. Are blinds like these very expensive?"

"Yes, they cost a bit," said Percy. "But I can give you a very good price. How many would the sheik be considering?"

The sheik had to think a minute.

"Let's say twenty," he said.

"That's twenty single ones, you mean," said Percy.

"No, I mean twenty thousand," said the sheik. "Twenty thousand would do to start with."

Percy didn't say anything. He went a bit red about the ears.

And then he went over to a cardboard box and dug out his light-blue maths book.

"We might as well get a contract signed straight away," he said.

Ulf sat on the bed and watched them calculate and do writing in ink. After a while they were done. They had both written their names on the paper. Then they stood up and shook hands.

"Shouldn't you smoke a cigar now?" asked Ulf.

Percy had told him that was what you did when you did business.

"That's right, Ulf," said Percy. "I almost forgot."

He opened the door. He called out louder than Frank Sinatra.

"Dad!" he called. "Dad! We don't need to move! Come here straight away and bring your biggest business cigar!"

It took a moment before Percy's father came. They could hear his shoes in the hall. And he started talking way before he got to Percy's room.

"You have to stop this nonsense, Percy," he said. "You know it doesn't help anything. We've talked about it thousands of times."

But when he got to the door he went quiet.

First he stared at the interpreter and the sheik. Then he stared at Percy who was standing in the middle of the room holding up a torn-out piece of maths paper.

"What in the name of peace is going on here?" he said.

"Percy has just done the deal of a lifetime," said Ulf.

When the sheik had smoked his cigar and Percy's father had turned the piece of paper over a thousand times at least, and said that Percy was a genius, they went out to the car. By that time Frank Sinatra had changed songs. Now he was singing, *You make me feel so young.*

This time the sheik also sat in the front seat. Ulf and Percy draped themselves in the back seat, feeling better than they had for ages.

"Now it is time to go back again," said the sheik.

"Yes, it's time for the coconut balls," said Ulf.

So they drove through the streets of Stureby. The wind ruffled their hair. The motor hummed beautifully. Now and then Ulf would point out the sights. He pointed to the sweet shop, the chestnut tree and the worst hill for going fast on your go-kart.

Lasse, Charlie, Olle Rickberg, Bjorn and all the others were standing outside Karlsson's paint shop. They were standing on the pavement and they waved as they drove past.

A bit further on, there was a girl with light blond hair, braces and a fluffy jersey.

"Stop!" said Ulf. "Can we stop here for a minute?"

The car stopped beside Marianne.

"Hi," said Ulf. "Aren't you with Arne?"

"No," she said. "I got tired of him. He only wants to play the washboard. He's boring. And he doesn't kiss very well."

"Then maybe we can see each other later?" said Ulf.

"Yes, of course we can," she said.

The car drove on. When they got back to Ulf's house

the sheik put up the hood, because it was getting dark. Then Percy pinched Ulf on the shoulder.

"Thanks for today," he said. "Today was a good day."

"It will be a good day tomorrow, too," said Ulf.

Also by Ulf Stark

My *friend Percy's*
magical gym shoes

When Ulf gets a new classmate,
everything changes. Percy can
do anything, thanks to his magical
gym shoes. Ulf wants the shoes,
so he too can be brave and
strong – and he'll pay anything
to get them.

'A very, very nuanced portrait of a friendship ...'
Kate de Goldi, *Saturday Morning with Kim Hill*, Radio New Zealand

'a humorous slice of Swedish life ...'
Otago Daily Times

'The author could make it sound, when Ulf was talking, that
he was saying something sad and funny at the same time ...'
Younger Readers' review, *Northern Advocate*

'... captures both the vulnerability and the egocentricity of
childhood ...'
Booknotes

Can you whistle, Johanna?
Why doesn't Berra have a grandfather?
How can he get one?
There are plenty of old men at the
retirement home, Ulf suggests.
They go there together to find one –
ideally one who eats pigs' trotters,
invites you to tea and can teach you
to whistle.

*Winner of the Deutscher Jugendliteraturpreis, awarded to authors
of children's and teenage literature for outstanding works.*

'A sweetly poignant tale that brings both laughter and tears.
Highly recommended.'
  Otago Daily Times

'… a gentle account of companionship and loss, beautifully
illustrated, funny and sad.'
  Good Morning Show

'*Can you whistle, Johanna?* is a treasure.'
  Magpies

'Stark's understated humour combines with the deceptive
simplicity of his prose to create a charming story … Highly
recommended.'
  Booknotes